THE PRINCESS WITH THE BLAZING BOTTOM

by BEACH

Sir Wayne and Dragon were out exploring –
Rocketing, rolling, swooping and soaring.

Higher and higher they climbed through the sky
When all of a sudden . . .

THE PRINCESS WITH THE BLAZING BOTTOM

A VERY FIERY FAIRY TALE

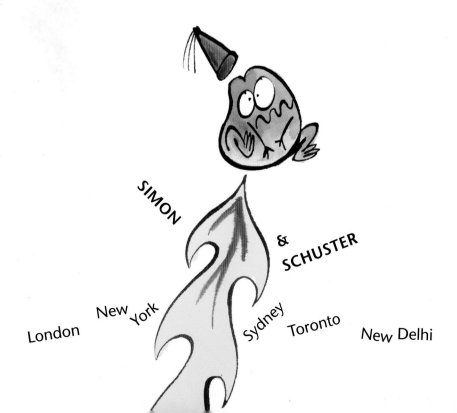

SIMON & SCHUSTER

London   New York   Sydney   Toronto   New Delhi

For Lucy, James & Katie

Edited by Polly Whybrow &

Designed by Emily Hearn

Simon & Schuster
First published in Great Britain in 2023 by Simon & Schuster UK Ltd
1st Floor, 222 Gray's Inn Road, London, WC1X 8HB
Text & illustration copyright © 2023 Beach
The right of Beach to be identified as the author and illustrator of this
work has been asserted by him in accordance with the Copyright,
Designs and Patents Act, 1988 • All rights reserved,
including the right of reproduction in whole or in part in any form
A CIP catalogue record for this book is available
from the British Library upon request
ISBNs: 978-1-3985-2530-6 (HB) 978-1-4711-9728-4 (PB)
978-1-4711-9727-7 (eB)
Printed in China
1 3 5 7 9 10 8 6 4 2

FSC
www.fsc.org
MIX
Paper | Supporting
responsible forestry
FSC® C144853

. . . Sir Wayne heard a cry.

Far down below, a girl was waving.
"A Princess!" said Wayne. "And I think she needs saving!

Just look at that terrible creature beneath her.
That smile! Those teeth! It's trying to eat her!"

"Hold on, your Highness – Sir Wayne's on his way.
I can battle that beast and save the day!

Nothing will stop me –
I'll climb every wall.

No moat is too deep,

no tower too tall . . .

I'll swish and I'll swash and I'll fight on and on.

No beast can defeat
a knight this strong!"

"Oh please," said Dragon, "do give it a rest.
When it comes to a rescue,
we all know who's best.

Just look at this body – so muscly and lean.

Sir Wayne shook his head.
"A dragon's alright . . .

But you can't beat a knight when it comes to a fight."

Then he charged at the beast with his sword held high
And aimed a great blow at its huge middle eye.

BOINK! went his sword.

BING!

BANG!

BONK! went Sir Wayne.

His hat split in half and his suit did the same.

"Told you," said Dragon. "A knight's not enough.
You need something tough when the going gets rough.
Something bigger and badder and one of a kind.

Something,"
said Dragon . . .

"...With a blazing behind!"

He smiled at the beast. "Your fun here is done.
One bottom blast and this battle is won."

So he charged at full speed, flying fast and low,
Aimed at the beast and let his bottom blow.

But what came next was less than he hoped.
Three pops,

two sparks

and a small
puff of smoke.

The beast licked his lips. "What a dreadful shame.
All that showing off must have used up your flame.

Never mind," he smiled, "I like my dragons cold.
Perfect with ketchup and a knight not-so-bold."

"Blazing boots!" cried Dragon. "This looks like the end!
I'm sorry," he sobbed, "I'm a terrible friend."

"No, it's me," wept Wayne, "I'm the worst knight ever.
I can't fight alone – I should have known better."

But just when it seemed the end was nigh . . .

. . . The princess herself called down from up high.

"Would you mind," she asked, "if I fight the beast?
A proper princess should get one go at least."

"You?!" laughed the beast. "You can't possibly win!
You can't beat a beast because Daddy's a king."

"No," she replied, taking aim at her wagon.
"But I can beat a beast . . ."

"... Because Mummy's a DRAGON!"

"You're half dragon?!" the beast gasped. "How can this be?!"
But the half that was dragon was plain to see.

As our twirling princess finished her jump

With a tail-waving, trail-blazing, fight-saving . . .

The beast turned and fled – our friends gave a cheer,
"Hooray for the girl with the right royal rear!"

"So blazing!" said Dragon. "So brave!" said Sir Wayne.
"The best combination of courage and flame."

So now Princess Fireball has joined our crew
And Dragon and Wayne have learnt something new:

When you want to fire flames that really impress –

Nothing can beat a blazing Princess.